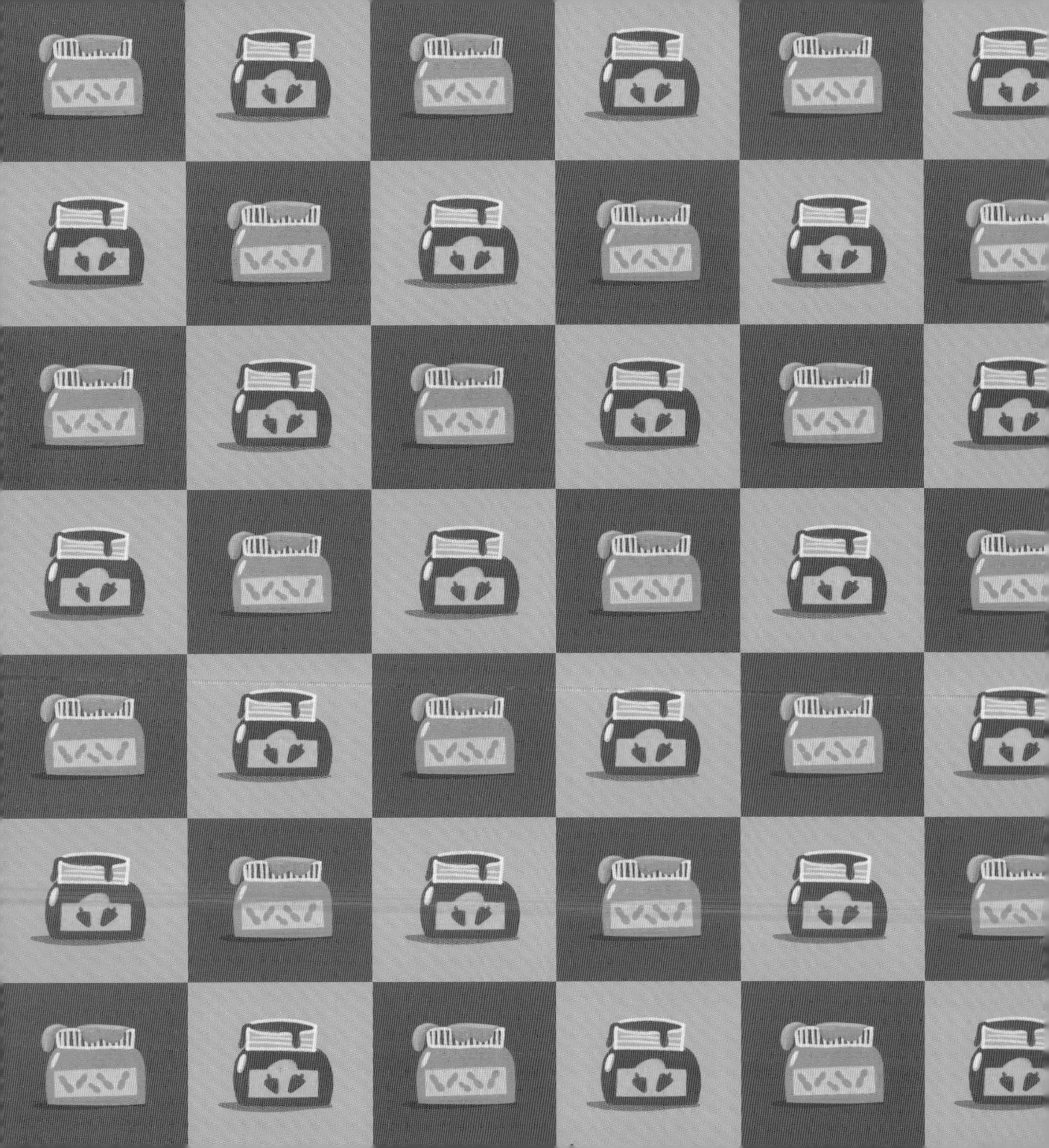

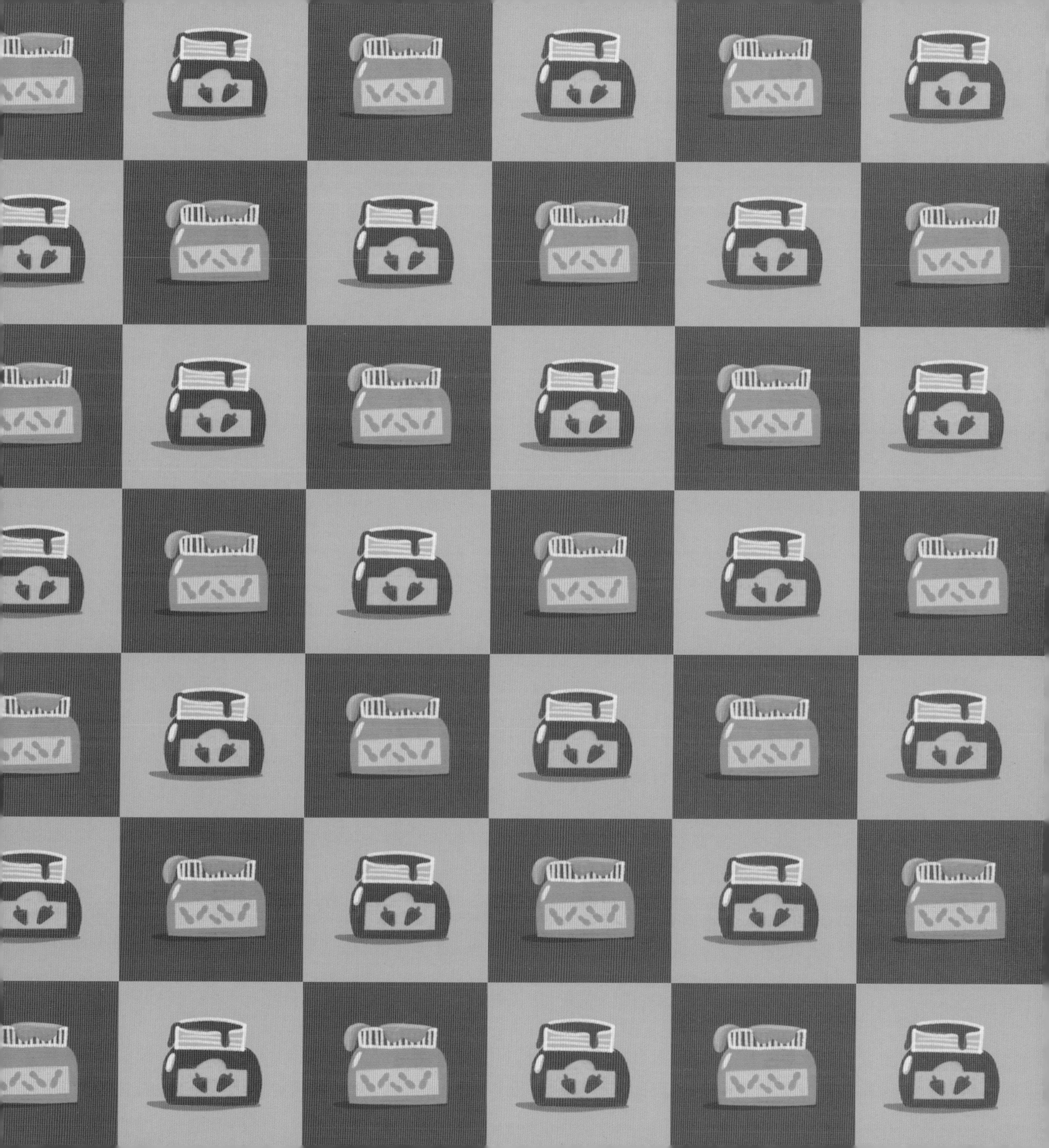

IMAGINE THAT™

Licensed exclusively to Imagine That Publishing Ltd
Tide Mill Way, Woodbridge, Suffolk, IP12 1AP, UK
www.imaginethat.com
Copyright © 2020 Imagine That Group Ltd
All rights reserved
2 4 6 8 9 7 5 3 1
Manufactured in China

Written by Cece Graham
Illustrated by Róisín Hahessy

ISBN 978-1-78958-584-1

A catalogue record for this book is available from the British Library

DRAGONS LOVE PEANUT BUTTER and JAM

Written by Cece Graham

Illustrated by Róisín Hahessy

Not many people have ever
met a real-life dragon.

This is a dragon.

'Hello!'

Dragons have giant claws and fiery roars.

Their burps can be quite dangerous!

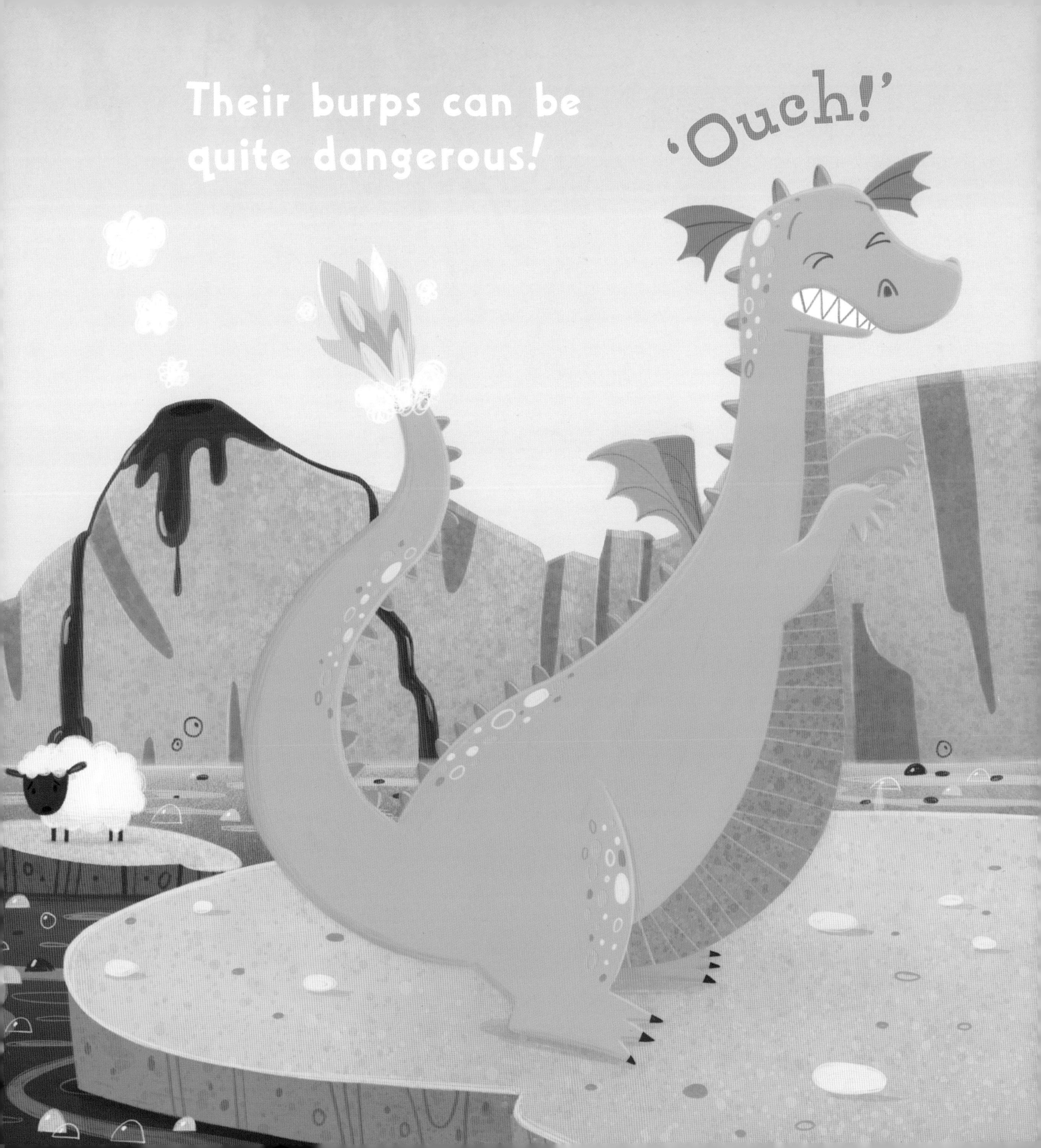

Some people get dinosaurs
and dragons mixed up.

'Hello!'

Dragons don't like
this very much.

Dragons think they are nothing like dinosaurs at all.

'We are not extinct,' said one dragon.

'We live in children's imaginations,' said another dragon.

'We do not move slowly on the ground,' said one dragon.

`We can
loop-the-loop
through the air,'
said another dragon.

'We do not have tiny brains,' said one dragon.

'We like word puzzles and maths, too,' said another dragon.

'Dinosaurs are
not magical,'
said one dragon.

'Dragons are the most magical creatures of all,' said another dragon.

'We do not eat other dragons,' said one dragon.

'Yum!'

'We LOVE to eat peanut butter and jam!' said another dragon.

'Laugh!'

'Giggle!'

`Do dragons really love peanut butter and jam?´ asked a passing sheep.

'Gulp!'

'Don't be ridiculous!'
said one dragon.

`Dragons love eating sheep,´ said another dragon.

Not many people have ever met a real-life dragon,

but they are much funnier than dinosaurs!

'Goodbye!'

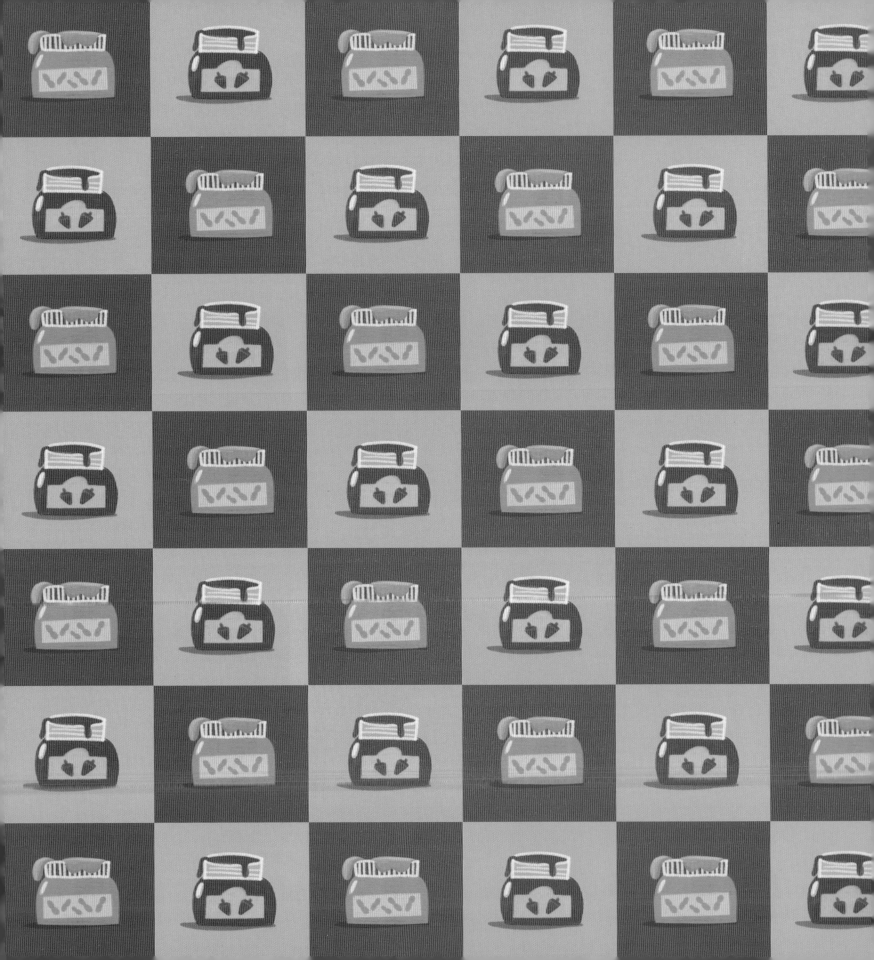